Contents

Meet the Characters

Aisha and Emily are best friends from Spellford Village. Aisha loves sports, whilst Emily's favourite thing is science. But what both girls enjoy more than anything is visiting Enchanted Valley and helping their unicorn friends, who live there.

Quickhoof

The four Sports and Games Unicorns help to make games and competitions fun for everyone. Quickhoof uses her magic locket to help players work well as a team.

Feeling confident in your skills and abilities is so important for sporting success. Brightblaze's magic helps to make sure everyone believes in themselves!

Brightblaze

Fairtail

Games are no fun when players cheat or don't follow the rules. Fairtail's magic locket reminds everyone to play fair!

When things get difficult, Spiritmane's perseverance locket gives sportspeople the strength to face their challenges and succeed.

Spiritmane

An Enchanted Valley lies a twinkle away,
Where beautiful unicorns live, laugh and play
You can visit the mermaids, or go for a ride,
So much fun to be had, but dangers can hide!

Your friends need your help ~ this is how you know:
A keyring lights up with a magical glow.
Whirled off like a dream, you won't want to leave.
Friendship forever, when you truly believe.

Chapter One
Schoolroom Nerves

Aisha Khan stood outside her classroom door with her best friend Emily Turner, wishing she was anywhere else in the world.

"I don't know if I can do this," she whispered.

Emily squeezed her hand comfortingly

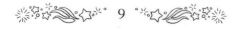

and said, "It's only a book report."

Aisha fiddled with the bookmark in her copy of *Black Beauty*.

The two friends both loved the book. They must have read it a hundred times. But while Emily felt confident in the classroom, Aisha was more at home outside on the sports fields. This book report was giving her butterflies in her tummy.

She groaned and leaned against the wall. "I wish Black Beauty would come so I could ride away!"

Emily put her hand on Aisha's shoulder. "There's a special trick you can do if nothing else is working. Shall I tell you?"

"OK," Aisha whispered.

Emily said, "When you're feeling nervous, just imagine something funny!"

"Like what?"

"How about Miss Mayhew dressed as a clown? You'll feel much better, I promise."

Aisha frowned. "I'm not sure that'll work. But I'll try."

Just then a bright twinkling caught Emily's eye. There was a light shining out of Aisha's pocket. Aisha was so anxious she hadn't even noticed!

"Aisha, your keyring's glowing!" Emily pulled her own keyring out. "And so is mine!"

A big, relieved grin spread across Aisha's face.

"This is even better than Black Beauty

coming to rescue me," she said. "We're off to Enchanted Valley for another adventure!"

When their unicorn-shaped crystal keyrings glowed, it meant the girls' unicorn friend, Queen Aurora, was calling them to come and visit. Aurora ruled over Enchanted Valley, a magical kingdom

filled with unicorns and all kinds of other wonderful creatures. Emily and Aisha had travelled there many times.

Neither of them was worried about missing their presentation because no time passed in the real world while the girls were in Enchanted Valley. But they couldn't just disappear in the middle of a school corridor – someone might see.

Round the corner there was a big bookcase, full of picture books for the youngest children. Emily and Aisha quickly ducked behind it. They touched their keyrings together.

Instantly, rainbow-coloured sparkles rushed up and whirled around them. Aisha and Emily rose up off the floor as the magical sparkles swirled and glittered, dancing in the air.

A moment later, they sank gently back down to the ground. When the sparkles faded, the school corridor had vanished. Now they were standing on the lush green grass of Enchanted Valley!

They looked around and saw they were outside Queen Aurora's beautiful castle. Its towers, twisty and golden like unicorn horns, rose up into a clear blue sky. On the hill beyond the castle stood the huge silver stadium where the Enchanted Valley Games would soon be held. It was a special event in which the creatures of the valley would compete in every sport and game imaginable!

Queen Aurora came trotting over the
palace drawbridge to meet them. Her
coat shimmered with all the warm and
radiant colours of the dawn. Around her
neck hung her magical Friendship locket,
and a little crown sat on her head. Emily

and Aisha both gave her a big hug.

"Hello, Emily and Aisha! It's lovely to see you again!" Aurora said, whisking her golden tail with happiness.

"It's lovely to see you too," said Aisha, pressing her cheek against Aurora's. She felt so much better now she was here with her unicorn friend.

Emily asked, "Is everything OK? Has Selena caused more trouble?"

The wicked unicorn, Selena, who wanted to take Aurora's place as queen, was always causing problems. Last time Emily and Aisha visited Enchanted Valley, Selena had stolen the magical lockets from the Sports and Games Unicorns. The girls had helped Quickhoof get her

Teamwork locket back, but they still needed to find Brightblaze's Confidence locket, Fairtail's Sportsmanship locket and Spiritmane's Perseverance locket.

"Selena is refusing to give the lockets back unless we make her the new queen," Queen Aurora said. "Don't worry. We will never let that happen. But Selena's timing is especially bad just now."

Emily looked across to the stadium, where colourful flags were fluttering in the wind. "Of course. The Enchanted Valley Games are about to start!"

Aisha had a terrible thought. "You're not cancelling the Games because of the stolen lockets, are you?"

"I bet Selena would love it if that

happened," Emily scowled.

"Indeed she would," Aurora said. "We're not cancelling, but we are postponing the Games until we get the lockets back."

Aisha and Emily both frowned. "That's such a shame," said Emily.

"Don't be downhearted," Aurora said with a secretive smile. "We're still sports mad here. In fact, practice is about to start for one very special event."

The girls brightened.

"I called you both to Enchanted Valley because I thought you might like to watch the kelpies racing," said Aurora.

"What's a kelpie?" both girls asked at the same time.

"You'll see!" laughed Aurora. "Climb on

my back, and we'll be there in a flash!"

The girls didn't wait to be asked twice. Eagerly, they jumped on to Aurora's back.

The majestic unicorn gave two graceful bounds, and flew up into the air. They went soaring high above the hills and forests. Moments later, Emily and Aisha saw an astonishing sight. In the middle of a green meadow was a gigantic building shaped like a blue whale! A jet of water was shooting up from its blowhole and running down its sides.

As Aurora flew them closer, they saw the whale was actually see-through. Emily soon realised what it was.

"I can see swimming pools inside the whale!" she cried. "Loads of them. And they're really big ones!"

"Welcome to the Swimsplash Arena!"
Aurora announced.

Chapter Two
The Swimsplash Arena

"It's the finest swimming playpark in all of Enchanted Valley," Queen Aurora said, as the girls clung tightly to her mane. "This is where we're going to hold the swimming events when the Games begin."

They landed at the front, just by the whale's huge smiling mouth. Goblins, animals and many magical creatures were all hurrying inside through the mouth, holding their rolled-up towels and swimming costumes.

"In we go!" said Aurora.

The girls jumped off Aurora's back and walked hand in hand into the Swimsplash Arena. They looked around in wonder. This was better than any water park in the real world, by miles!

There were swimming pools, of course – deep ones and shallow ones – but that wasn't all. At the back, near the whale's tail, was an extra-deep pool with a diving board where an otter in swimming goggles was getting ready to jump. To one side was a special fun zone, where twisty slides and tubes led into the water. Lots of creatures were having a noisy, splashy time there. A group of young pixies were soaking one another and laughing, while nearby a family of penguins lined up to dive in one by one. On the other side was a peaceful zone, with wave pools where several creatures were relaxing as the water washed back and forth over them. Two pufflebunnies waved from rubber tyres as they floated past down a lazy river.

Even the little baby creatures were included. They had a bubble garden, safely behind a barrier, where they could crawl about and play with Bubble Blasters – water pistols that fired streams

of bubbles instead of water. There were gentle little waterfalls and fountain jets, as well as toys for them to play with.

"There's a café too," said Emily, pointing. "'The Babbling Brook'. Imagine playing in the pools all day and then going for a milkshake afterwards!"

"Or a hot chocolate," said Aisha. "This place is wonderful!"

Aurora smiled. "Glad you like it! Look, our friends are here already."

In a pool decorated with seashells, Pearl the mermaid was swimming. She waved across at Aisha and Emily, who waved back. A group of other mermaids popped their heads up out of the water and waved too.

"I'm not surprised to see Pearl here,"
Emily said. "All this water. She must love
it!"

"And there's Prism the Rainbow
Parrot," added Aisha. "Hi, Prism!"

Prism came swooping down in a flurry
of shining colours. He wrapped his wings
around Aisha and Emily in a big friendly
hug. "Hello, you two! Great to see you
again."

"Are you here to swim?" Emily asked.
She wasn't sure if parrots liked swimming.

"Oh, I'm here because of the slide
races," said Prism proudly. "They'll be
part of the Enchanted Valley Games."

"*Slide* races?" exclaimed Aisha.

"First one into the water wins!"

explained Prism.

"Slide races sound so cool," said Emily.

"And I'm in charge of making the slides," Prism said. "Watch this!'

He spread his wings wide. A rainbow shone out, created by Prism's own special magic. The girls looked on in amazement as the rainbow trail went up and along, then curled in a gentle spiral down into the water.

Aurora waved her horn, and a glimmer of magic sparkled through the air. Prism closed his wings, but the rainbow didn't vanish like it usually did. Aurora's magic made it stay!

Prism bowed, sweeping his wings. "Hey presto! One magical rainbow water slide.

And because they're magic, you can slide up them as well as down!"

Aisha and Emily looked at each other in delight and clapped their hands.

"Why don't we go and find Brightblaze?" Queen Aurora suggested. "She's trying to give everyone confidence before the races, but she's finding it hard without her locket. I think she'd be glad to have some help."

Emily, Aisha and Aurora found Brightblaze the Confidence unicorn by the racing pool. Her body was a gorgeous pearly colour, and her mane and tail were scarlet. She was bending her head down, talking to a group of bluish-green horses who were neck-deep in the water.

"Wow!" Aisha said. "I didn't think horses could swim."

"They can, actually," Emily said. "Swimming is a brilliant way for a horse to get exercise, especially when it's recovering from an injury."

Aurora chuckled. "That's right, Emily. Just one thing, though. Those aren't horses."

"Really?" Emily exclaimed.

"They're the kelpies I've brought you to meet!" Aurora said.

As the girls came closer, they saw the creatures they'd thought were horses had two forelegs with hooves, but fish tails instead of hind legs. Their manes were made of trailing seaweed, not slimy but fine, like green silk.

"How cool!" Aisha said in awe.

The kelpies lined up at one end of the pool, each one in a lane. Brightblaze gave them the signal to start. They thrashed their tails and galloped with their front hooves. Waves washed out and foam flew up as the creatures powered through the water. They seemed completely at home there, moving as fast underwater as normal horses could on land. It was a thrilling sight!

Aurora and the girls said hello to Brightblaze, who seemed nervous.

"It's good to see you," she said. "I just wish I had my locket back! The Games are due to start very soon, you know.

How am I supposed to give everyone confidence when I haven't even got my locket?"

The girls and the unicorns were showered with water as one of the kelpies suddenly popped his head up. "Hellooo,

you two!" he bellowed. "Oops, sorry about that. Call me Eddie. Kelpie team captain!"

"Hi, Eddie!" the girls said.

"Now, don't you fret about that locket, Brightblaze," Eddie said. "I can give my team a rousing pep talk, and they'll be all fired up with confidence. You'll see."

"I hope he's right," Aisha whispered to Emily. "Poor Brightblaze does look nervous."

Eddie turned to Aisha and Emily. "Now, you two. I've got a very important question to ask you."

"Go on," said Aisha.

In a serious voice, Eddie asked, "Do you like swimming?"

Both the girls laughed. "Of course," they said. "We love it."

Eddie gave them a truly enormous grin. "Well, what are you waiting for? Jump on in!"

Emily and Aisha looked at one another, both thinking the same thing. They were still dressed in school uniform! They couldn't jump into a swimming pool like this!

But just then Aurora waggled her horn. Sparkling twinkles danced in the air and next moment, Aisha and Emily found they were wearing shiny purple swimsuits.

"That's better," Aurora said with a smile.

Emily and Aisha got ready to jump in. But then—

Kaboom!

A crash of thunder echoed across the arena. The girls turned to see where it had come from. A bright flash of lightning lit up all the pools. Then came a high whinnying laugh that the girls knew only too well. A silvery unicorn appeared on the high diving board, prancing and gloating. Creatures ran in fright at the sight of her.

Emily shuddered. "Oh, no! It's Selena!"

Chapter Three
Selena Shows Her Face

Selena stood at the top of the high
diving platform. She sneered down at the
creatures who were scattering out of the
way. Next to her was a lumpy-looking
creature with big arms, pointy ears and
greyish skin. He was wearing a baggy,
stripy swimming suit.

"It's Grubb!" said Aisha. The ogre was Selena's latest henchman.

"And look what he's got round his neck," Emily said. "It's Brightblaze's locket!"

Grubb stomped to the end of the diving

board. Even though he was really high up, he didn't seem scared at all. "Hello down there!" he bellowed.

Down below, the creatures went into a panic. Mermaids, pixies, goblins and even otters all crowded to the edges of the pool. Some of them scrambled out of the water as fast as they could. Others just huddled there, quivering in fear.

Selena laughed out loud to see the uproar. "Well, now! You two silly little girls may have got the better of me last time by winning back the Teamwork locket, but guess what? I've still got the other three lockets!" She tilted her head and smiled as sweetly as she could. "I'm willing to give them back, of course, on one teeny-weeny little condition ..."

"You want to be queen," said Emily.

"That's right!" trilled Selena. "Come on,
Aurora. Give me your crown, bow down
to me, and your Games can go ahead!"

"Never!" shouted Aurora.

Aisha folded her arms and glared.
"Aurora's the queen of Enchanted Valley
and she always will be!"

"Oh, is that so?" Selena smirked. "Look!
I've given Grubb the Confidence locket.
You'll never be able to take it from him.
You haven't got the nerve!"

Grubb the ogre jumped up and down
on the diving board, which went *wubba-
wubba-wubba* like a ruler twanged on
the edge of a school desk. He shouted,

"CANNON
BAAAALLLLL!"
And he jumped.

All the creatures
around the diving
pool squealed and
cowered away.

Grubb curled
up into a ball as
he plummeted
through the air.

Next second:
splathooooom!
He plunged into
the diving pool like
a boulder.

A massive spray

of water shot up and out. Almost the entire diving pool emptied itself over the Swimsplash Arena – and everyone inside it!

The spectators up in the stands howled as water crashed over them. Queen Aurora caught a gush of water in the face and blinked. Even the baby creatures crawling around in the bubble garden got splashed. From one end of the arena to the other, creatures were soaked to the skin. A few of them tried to duck behind tables or behind signs, but they got drenched all the same.

The water steadily began to flood back into the diving pool. Dripping creatures began to look around for dry towels and

wring out their sodden clothes.

"Selena's disappeared!" Aisha exclaimed, peering up at where the silver unicorn had been moments ago.

Emily scanned the arena. "You're right, there's no sign of her."

Grubb was still there, however. He was running around the arena in his baggy swimsuit, calling out to all the frightened creatures and making faces at them.

"Grubb, be careful!" Queen Aurora called out. "You mustn't run by the pool. You'll slip and hurt yourself!"

Grubb stuck out his tongue and blew a raspberry. "Me, fall over? Ha! That'll never happen!" And away he went, running even faster than before.

Just then, they heard a cry. "We want to get out! Help! We're scared to swim!"

In the racing pool three goblin children were floating, holding on to a big inflatable toadstool. The massive wave from Grubb's cannonball had washed them right into the middle of the pool, and now they couldn't reach the side.

"Hold on!" called Emily.

"We're coming!" Aisha added.

They sat on the side and slid down into the water. As soon as they were in, a shiver struck Emily, even though the water wasn't cold. "It looks very deep," she said, nervously.

Beside her, Aisha held on tightly to the edge of the pool.

"I'm scared to let go," she said.

"Me too!" said Emily. "What's going on? We usually love swimming."

"Oh dear, girls. I think you've lost your confidence," Aurora said sadly.

"And Grubb has way too much," said Emily. "Look at him!"

She pointed to Grubb, who was pounding his chest like a gorilla.

"Help us!" wailed the three little goblins together.

But the girls were just too nervous to leave the side.

"Let's ask the kelpies for help," Aisha suggested.

The girls climbed out of the water and shuffled over to where the kelpies had been practising. But when they reached the kelpies, they found them clinging on to the sides. Their eyes were all big and wide and their teeth were chattering.

"Those goblins are stuck. Can you help?" Aisha asked, pointing towards the three scared little goblins.

"I'm sorry," said a kelpie, shaking her head. "I swim every day, but I just *can't* face swimming now."

"Oh dear, Grubb's stolen *everyone's* confidence!" Aisha said to Emily.

"Not quite everyone!" said a familiar voice.

It was Eddie!

With a huge flick of his tail, the brave kelpie rocketed towards the helpless goblins. He swam up to the inflatable toadstool that they were all clinging to. Using his nose, he pushed it through the water and kept swimming until it was safely at the pool's edge.

Brightblaze, Aurora and the girls helped the very relieved goblin children out of

the pool. "Let's take them to the Babbling Brook Café," Aurora said. "They need to get warm and dry!"

They hurried over to the café. A purple flamingo wearing a tall white chef's hat opened the door for them. "Welcome! I'm Lofty," he said. He looked down at the little goblins. "In you come, quickly now!"

Soon everyone was sitting together in a comfy corner, with plenty of soft cushions to rest on. Lofty went to get some magical air-blowers that looked like spinning paper windmills on straws. The air they blew out was wonderfully warm and dried everyone off in no time.

"Now how about some hot chocolate?" Lofty said.

"Yes please!" they all said.

Moments later they were sipping on big mugs of frothy hot chocolate with marshmallows in it. It warmed them up from the inside like a radiator, and Emily and Aisha soon felt much better.

Lots of other creatures had taken refuge

inside the café, to hide away from Grubb. Lofty did what he could to cheer them up with warm towels and hot drinks. It was getting quite crowded!

"OK," said Brightblaze, when she finished her drink. "Let's go and get my locket back from Grubb. This has gone on long enough!"

Queen Aurora stood up to leave, but all the little creatures huddled up to her, whimpering with fear. "Don't go!" they begged. "What if scary Selena comes back?"

"You'd better stay here in the café and look after everyone," Emily told Queen Aurora.

"And we'll help Brightblaze find her

locket!" added Aisha.

The three of them headed back to the pool. Grubb put his hands up to his ears and waggled them. "You'll never catch me!" he yelled, and off he went, running around the pool.

The girls started to chase after Grubb, but the poolside was still awash with water from his divebomb. It was so slippery, they had to walk slowly just to stay safe. Meanwhile, Grubb had run all the way round to the far side of the pool.

"We'll never catch him like this," Aisha groaned. "Brightblaze, can you fly after him?"

"I would," Brightblaze said, "but … I'm not feeling very confident about flying right now. What if I hit the ceiling? What if you fall off?"

Brightblaze's confidence had gone, too.

And without it, they'd never get her locket back, and Selena would win!

Chapter Four
Bubble Trouble

Emily looked around to see if there was anything nearby that could help them.

Next to the café was the Bubble Garden. All the little creatures who had been playing there had dropped their toys and run inside the café to hide. There were brightly coloured toys like water pistols lying around.

"What are those?" Emily asked Brightblaze.

"Bubble Blasters," the unicorn explained.

Emily rubbed her chin thoughtfully. "Hmm. What if we baffled Grubb with some bubbles?"

"Let's try it!" Aisha said. She went and grabbed a Bubble Blaster and passed one to Emily.

The three of them crouched down behind a tall plastic plant with lots of green fronds hanging down.

Grubb was doing another lap of the pool. He was coming in their direction.

Brightblaze shook with nerves as he

stomped towards them. "Get ready to babble Grubb with the buffles!" she said through chattering teeth.

Aisha and Emily turned the power dials on their Bubble Blasters all the way up to eleven.

"Now!" Emily yelled.

The girls jumped out from their hiding

place, aimed their Bubble Blasters at Grubb — and fired.

An amazing stream of bubbles shot out. In seconds they were as thick as a snowstorm. The girls could hardly see their hands in front of their faces for all the bubbles in the air. It was like being dunked in a gigantic glass of lemonade!

Grubb flapped his arms about, trying to clear the bubbles away. "I can't see!" he bellowed. "What's all this?" A bubble flew up his nose and he sneezed.

"Quick, grab the locket!" Aisha called to Emily.

Emily looked around, and saw nothing but swirling bubbles. "I can't see it," she said. "I can't even see Grubb!"

They heard him blundering about for
a few moments, then there was a sudden,
heavy splash.

"He's fallen in!" Aisha said.

As one by one the bubbles popped
and the girls slowly became able to see
again, they saw Grubb bobbing about in

the pool. He looked quite pleased with himself.

"We ought to jump in and catch him!" said Emily.

"Come on, then," Aisha said.

The girls looked at one another nervously, then reached to hold each other's hands. This wasn't how swimming usually went for them at all. Normally they couldn't wait to get into the water. But now, the pool looked deep, cold and frightening.

"Don't worry, girls!" Eddie called over from the racing pool. "I'll get the scallywag. I'll teach him to scare *my* friends!"

Eddie began to swim towards the pool's

edge, going very fast. Then, like a leaping salmon, he launched himself out of the water. He flew through the air, turned a full somersault, and splashed down in the big pool next to a very surprised Grubb.

"Hooray for Eddie!" cheered the girls and Brightblaze.

Grubb doggy-paddled away as fast as

he could, while Eddie churned up the water swimming after him.

"Eddie was so confident to begin with that it looks like the missing locket hasn't affected him!" said Brightblaze.

As they watched Eddie chase Grubb in the pool, they suddenly heard a voice calling, "Emily! Aisha! Over here!"

They looked over to see their mermaid friend Pearl waving at them. Pearl and the other mermaids were all swimming in the Glitter Grotto, a special pool decorated with sparkly coral and shiny stones. The girls and Brightblaze went hurrying over.

"We've had an idea," Pearl said. "We think we can help!"

"How?" Emily asked.

"Mermaid magic!" Pearl grinned. She took a beautiful coral comb out of her hair.

Emily's eyes went wide as she remembered. "Of course. If a human wears a mermaid comb, they can breathe underwater and swim like a fish!"

"Yes!" Aisha agreed. "Maybe swimming won't seem so scary if we can breathe underwater, just like mermaids do."

They took a comb each and ran back to the pool, where Eddie was still chasing Grubb around.

"Time to get that locket back!" Emily said. Aisha nodded firmly.

They reached up to slide the combs into their hair. Soon they'd have mermaid powers, and they'd teach that ogre a lesson …

But as he swam past, Grubb reached up and slapped Emily's comb out of her hand!

"Whoops-a-daisy!" he sneered. "Butterfingers!"

The comb flew through the air and landed with a *PLOP* – right in the

middle of the deep pool.

"Oh, no!" Aisha cried. "Your comb!"

Emily couldn't go into the pool without the comb, but she couldn't get the comb without going into the pool!

Emily groaned. "What on earth am I going to do now?"

Chapter Five
Mermaid Magic

Aisha took a deep breath. "I'm still feeling nervous about going anywhere near the water," she said. "But I've still got *my* mermaid comb. So I think … maybe … I can get your comb back."

Emily gave Aisha a tight hug. "I *know* you can!" she said.

Aisha gulped. "OK. Here we go," she said. "Wish me luck!"

She quickly slid the comb into her hair. Before she had time to worry about it, she threw herself into the water.

Emily cheered, "Go on, Aisha!"

Aisha gasped and spluttered. The water began to swirl around her in a mini whirlpool. It carried her with it, spinning her in a circle, faster and faster like a skater on the ice.

A strange feeling was starting to creep into her toes and up through her feet. It was a sort of tingling, like when you come indoors after walking through the snow.

Her legs had disappeared completely.

Aisha had a mermaid tail!

Emily clapped delightedly. "It worked! Now you can swim! I believe in you!"

"Go, Aisha!" said Brightblaze, stamping her hooves.

"I'll do my best," Aisha promised.

The funny thing was, even with her new mermaid tail, she *still* didn't feel confident. Her mind was buzzing with all the things that could go wrong. What if the comb fell out? What if Grubb blocked her way?

Aisha made up her mind. She might be scared, but Emily was counting on her, and so were Queen Aurora and the whole kingdom. With a determined flick of her tail, she duck-dived down under the surface.

To her surprise, she could see underwater, just as if she was wearing swimming goggles. Her eyes weren't stinging at all. There were Grubb's legs kicking away, and there was Eddie chasing him. And there was Emily's comb, gleaming on the bottom of the pool.

Aisha swam for all she was worth. The water got cooler and darker the deeper she swam, and she started to feel scared.

Just as she was about to lose her nerve, she got to the bottom.

She reached down and grabbed Emily's comb. Holding it tightly, she flipped over and swam back the other way.

Emily and Brightblaze watched nervously from the side of the pool. Emily crossed her fingers for luck. Next moment, Aisha suddenly burst out of the water, waving the comb triumphantly in her hand.

"Well done, Aisha!" Emily cheered. "You did it!"

Aisha passed the comb up to Emily. "Come on in, and let's help Eddie catch Grubb."

Emily popped the comb into her hair.

She was about to jump into the pool, but before she could, Grubb jumped *out!*

"Get back here, you ruffian!" shouted Eddie from the water.

"Nah," said Grubb. "I've had enough. Bored now!"

And off he ran, whooping and skidding in the puddles.

Emily sighed in frustration. She took Aisha's outstretched hand and helped her to wriggle out of the pool. They both took the mermaid combs out of their hair, and, with a swirl of magic, Aisha's tail turned back into legs.

Eddie laid his long head on the poolside and stuck his bottom lip out. "Oh, barnacles and bladderwrack," he grumbled. "I wish I could come out of the water and help you!"

"I wish you could too, Eddie," said Aisha. "You're the only one of us who has any confidence left."

Emily peered over to the back of the Swimsplash Arena. "What's that rotten ogre up to now?"

Grubb was back at the diving pool.

Emily shuddered. "He's not going to do another cannonball, is he?"

Grubb climbed up the ladder to the very top, where the diving board was. The moment he reached it, the whole diving tower grew. It became taller and taller, rising like a magic beanstalk until it was right up to the ceiling!

"That's more like it!" Grubb laughed. "Nice and high! But not too high for me." He held the locket up. "I thought you wanted this?" he taunted the friends. "Come and get it!"

Emily and Aisha looked on in horror. The diving board had been frighteningly high up before. The thought of going

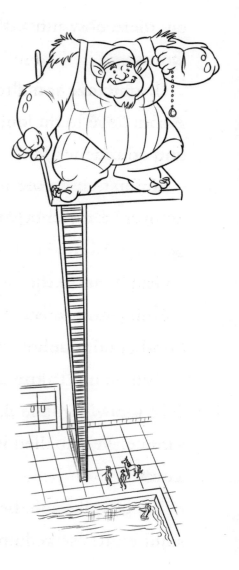

up there now made them go weak at the knees.

Brightblaze was shivering with fear. Aisha gave her a hug. "What's wrong?" she asked.

"I can't climb the ladder because of my hooves," Brightblaze said. "And I can't fly you up. All my confidence is gone. I'm too nervous to fly."

Emily and Aisha gripped one another's hands and squeezed tightly.

"We've got to try," Aisha said.

"I know," Emily agreed. "We've got no choice. We can't let Selena win. We just can't."

They walked to the bottom of the ladder and looked up. It stretched

 72

dizzyingly high above them.

"One step at a time," said Aisha.

"And whatever you do, don't look down," Emily added.

Aisha took the lead, Emily followed, and they began to climb. Grubb's mocking voice echoed in their ears, but they did their best to ignore him.

Rung by rung, they climbed up. Aisha's foot skidded on a wet rung and she stopped, clinging tight to the ladder and breathing hard, until she felt ready to go on again. Emily reassured her friend. "Almost there," she said. "Just keep going, nice and easy."

It was like being in an endless dream, climbing up a ladder but never seeming to reach the top. But finally, they pulled themselves on to the very highest platform. They clung to the safety rail for dear life. The tower was so high it seemed to wobble beneath them. They could have reached out to touch the glass ceiling!

Grubb was there waiting for them. He

folded his arms and said, "What a couple of babies. Fancy being scared of a little diving tower like this!"

He strode over to the ladder and gave it a kick. The ladder snapped clean off, and fell with a clattering crash to the ground far below!

Aisha gasped. "Grubb, *no!*"

Grubb laughed. "Only one way down now, girls. Cheerio!"

With that, he ran to the end of the diving board and dived right off. The girls watched him plummet through the air and splash in the pool below.

The diving pool seemed impossibly far down, like a blue flag fluttering on a distant white hill. They could just see

Grubb climb out of the pool and give a triumphant dance before racing off to cause more havoc.

"We're higher than a house up here," whispered Aisha.

"And the ladder's gone!" Emily whispered back.

"And we have to stop Grubb!" Aisha cried.

But unless they jumped, the girls were stuck.

Chapter Six
The Biggest Leap

"Hello up there!" called a voice from
below.

Aisha and Emily looked down and saw
Eddie, who was swimming in circles down
in the diving pool, his hooves galloping
ahead of him while his tail swished
behind. "Gosh, look at you both," he said.

"You made it all the way to the top! You're doing brilliantly!"

"It doesn't feel like it," Aisha called down.

"You'll be amazed at what you can do if you believe in yourselves," Eddie said, and grinned. "Shall I tell you a big secret about confidence?"

The girls nodded.

"It's always easier to feel confident if you're part of a team," Eddie said.

Aisha and Emily looked at each other.

"We *are* a team," Aisha said.

"Best friends," Emily agreed. She looked down. "I … I think maybe I *can* do it. But only if you're there with me."

"I was going to say the same thing!"

exclaimed Aisha.

"I'll be down here in the water when you land," Eddie said. "There's nothing to fear. I promise you that."

The girls held hands and walked to the end of the diving board. They took deep breaths.

"On three. OK?" Aisha said.

Emily nodded, holding Aisha's hand very tight. "One, two … *three!*"

At the exact same moment, they jumped.

As Emily fell, she thought, *This isn't so bad!*

And as Aisha plunged into the water, she thought, *Is it over already?*

The girls swam up to the surface. They

trod water, gasping for air. Eddie quickly swam up to them and they held on to his mane. That felt a lot better.

"Well done, girls!" he said. "See? You were scared, but you did it!"

Emily and Aisha hugged one another. "Thank you, Eddie!" they said together.

"We couldn't have done it without you cheering us on."

Meanwhile, Grubb was on the move again. The girls watched as he ran over to one of the twisty rainbow slides that Prism had made earlier. He stood at the bottom of the slide and paused.

"Selena told me I had to hide this locket," he said. "I'm brilliant at hiding things. Aha! This slide looks like a good place! They'll never find it in here."

The girls laughed. Aisha called out, "Silly Grubb! You're a bit too confident for your own good."

"Yeah," said Emily. "We love waterslides. We'll get that locket back easily!"

Grubb chuckled. "Oh? We'll see about

that." He waggled his fingers, calling on his ogre magic. The rainbow slide began to change.

It curled up on itself until it was a narrow pipe instead of a slide. Then it went twisting and curling all around the arena! It zoomed up and down in scary zigzags and finished with a long drop right into the middle of the pool.

Aisha and Emily stared at it. It hung in the air like a giant, crazy straw, defying gravity.

Grubb bellowed with laughter. "Now *that's* what I call a waterslide!"

He jumped into it, waving the locket as he vanished.

Brightblaze came over to the diving

pool. "Do you think you can get my locket back?" she asked anxiously.

Aisha and Emily gulped. Emily said, "I mean, we *normally* love waterslides ..."

"... but this one looks a bit too much!" Aisha finished.

Eddie gave each of them a boost out of the water with his nose. "I know you can do it," he said warmly. "All you have to do is believe in yourselves. Believe in each other!"

Aisha stroked his soft green seaweed mane. "Oh, Eddie, I wish you could come with us! You always know what to say."

Eddie looked back at his fish tail. "It's a pity I can't climb up to the waterslides. I'd just flollop about. Very funny to see, but not much use."

Emily thought about that for a moment. "I wonder ..."

She took out the coral comb that Pearl had given her before.

"Eddie," she said, "the comb turned Aisha's legs into a fish tail. Maybe with you it'll work the other way around."

Eddie beamed. "Let's give it a go!"

Emily tucked the comb into Eddie's mane. Water began to swirl around him, just like it had around Aisha before. In a flurry of foam and bubbles, Eddie's tail disappeared and two strong-looking horse legs took its place.

Brightblaze, Aisha and Emily helped Eddie scramble up and out of the pool.

He stood there on four legs, dripping, with a big smile on his face.

"Hooray!" they all cheered.

"This feels amazing!" Eddie roared happily. "It worked! Good thinking, Emily. Now for the locket!"

Chapter Seven
Waterslide Ride

Eddie tried to walk over to the slide, but his brand-new legs wobbled about under him. "Whoops!" he muttered, and tried again. He reminded Aisha of a newborn foal learning how to walk.

"Are you OK?" Brightblaze asked him.

"Takes a bit of getting used to, this," he

said. He slipped on a patch of wet floor
and his four legs skidded out in different
directions. "Whoa!"

Emily and Aisha helped him to stand up
again. "Just do your best," Emily said.

"That's the spirit," Eddie said, sounding

more cheerful. But Aisha noticed he was shivering all over.

Together, the four of them headed to the slide's entrance. There was a stack of double ring floats for people to ride in, and magical water was gushing inside.

Emily looked in. She had expected the slide to glow with bright, jolly colours, but Grubb's magic had changed all that. It was pitch black.

"Oh dear," Aisha said. "It's even scarier than I expected."

At least they had Eddie with them. Emily turned to ask him what they should do, but to her surprise, he had stopped in his tracks. It was like he'd been frozen in place.

"Can't do it," he said.

"Eddie!" Emily cried. "What's wrong?"

"I just can't face going on that slide," Eddie said. "These legs feel funny! I'm not used to them yet."

"We'll take the comb back out," Aisha suggested.

"You'll turn right back into a kelpie with a tail," said Emily, "and you can go down the slide that way."

Eddie hesitated. He looked down into the dark opening, and shook his seaweedy mane. "Sorry, girls. It's too much. I still can't do it."

Aisha knew she had to do something, or the locket would be lost for ever. She suddenly remembered Emily's advice

from when they were outside the classroom back in their world.

"We should just pretend the slide is something funny!" she said.

Emily said, "I know. Let's pretend we're going down a pipe in a sweet factory, and we're going to land in a big pile of marshmallows!"

"That *would* be funny." Aisha giggled.

Eddie looked a little happier.

"And we could pretend the floats are jelly rings," Brightblaze suggested.

"Ooh, yes, and the water is toffee sauce and we're little gummy bears! Yum!" said Emily.

Eddie smiled. "That does sound funny! You know ... I think I'll do it after all."

"Hooray!" the girls cheered.

Eddie took a deep breath and a step forward. "Righto, then. Into the sweetie tube we go, for Aurora and for Enchanted Valley."

Brightblaze wiggled her horn and it lit up, shining bright light all around. "Now the slide won't be so dark," she said.

They climbed into double ring floats, ready to slide. Aisha and Brightblaze went first, and Emily and Eddie followed on behind. Aisha gave one brave push, the float started to move up the magical slide, and they were off!

Brightblaze made little frightened noises as they went whooshing up the pipe. Aisha was nervous too, but reached

over and hugged her. They thundered
upwards, as fast as an underground
train, then without warning they were
rocketing down. Next moment they were
zooming up again! Aisha's tummy felt

very strange, like when the car went over
a speed bump back home.

They whooshed around a long curve.

Aisha tilted over in her seat. Then the pipe swung back the other way, and she nearly fell out.

"Remember, it's a sweetie factory!" she yelled. "There's going to be a lovely pile of marshmallows at the end."

Up ahead, something twinkled in the dark. Brightblaze's locket! It was dangling from the roof of the tunnel.

"I see the locket!" Aisha yelled. "Hold on!" As they rushed by, she reached up, grabbed for it … and missed! "No!"

"Don't worry, I'll try!" Emily yelled from behind. She stretched her arm up as high as she could. Her fingers knocked the locket off its hook, but she couldn't hold on to it.

The locket fell through the air and tumbled behind the float, out of Emily's reach.

Eddie quickly flipped his head back and caught the locket in his mouth!

"Yay!" they all cheered as they burst out of the tube and splashed down into the pool. Everyone laughed with relief. Eddie neighed with triumph and shook his long green mane.

"That was fun!" Brightblaze said.

"It was, wasn't it?" grinned Aisha.

And Emily joked, "Who wants to go again?"

Chapter Eight
Pool Party

Aisha took the locket out of Eddie's mouth and hung it around Brightblaze's neck.

Instantly she felt her confidence coming back. What on earth had she been so worried about? It was only a swimming pool – and she loved swimming!

"Come on, everyone!" Emily called to the creatures in the Babbling Brook Café. "You can get back in the water now."

"Let's have a pool party!" Aisha shouted.

With squeals of joy, all the creatures who had been hiding in the café came flooding back out.

The first ones ran up to the pool and just dived straight in. Others climbed up the rainbow slides and went scooting down into the water. The three little goblins jumped on to their inflatable toadstool and drifted across the pool with cries of "Wheee!"

Baby creatures splashed and giggled in the fountains and danced in streams of bubbles. Eddie's team of kelpies went racing up and down their lanes again, full of winning spirit. The whole Swimsplash Arena echoed to the sound of everyone having fun!

But suddenly thunder boomed and lightning flashed. There stood Selena, up on the diving platform again.

"What are you lot all doing back in the water?" she demanded.

Emily and Aisha looked around anxiously. They expected the creatures in the pool to scatter and hide, like they had before.

But strangely, none of them did. They all looked confidently up at Selena.

"Why aren't you scared, you pathetic fools?" Selena screeched.

But nobody so much as twitched. Not even the little goblins or the babies in the bubble garden looked scared.

Pearl the mermaid said, "We don't need to be scared of you with Aisha and Emily around. They'll never let you win, and we all know it!"

Selena stamped her hoof and glared at the girls. "You horrible, meddling little pests! And as for you, Grubb, you miserable failure … Grubb? Grubb! Wherever you're hiding, come out at ONCE!"

The girls spotted Grubb in the Bubble Garden, hiding in one of the plastic plants.

Selena shouted "GRUBB! Stop pretending to be a bush! I can see you!"

Grubb squeaked in fear, jumped up from behind the plant and ran away. He sprinted through the entrance of the Swimsplash Arena and vanished from sight.

Emily and Aisha giggled. "Looks like we've found something Grubb is scared of after all," Emily said.

"That's right," said Aisha. "Selena!"

"I'll be back," Selena scowled. "And I'll get my revenge on you all. Just you wait and see!" She vanished with another thunderous crash.

"Good riddance!" Eddie called and everyone cheered.

The pool party was the best Aisha and Emily had ever been to! They had swimming races, splashing competitions and slide races. They played pool volleyball, and the kelpies taught everyone how to play water polo.

Eventually, the girls started to feel tired – and their fingers and toes had gone all wrinkly from being in the water for so long!

They climbed out of the pool and headed to the Babbling Brook Café, where Lofty the flamingo chef was waiting with hot chocolate and Queen Aurora had the hot air blowers ready.

In moments they were dry and toasty warm. Queen Aurora's horn twinkled with magic, and the girls found themselves back in their school uniforms again.

They couldn't leave without saying goodbye to their new friend Eddie, so they sat to watch the kelpies practise racing. The kelpies zoomed through the water as fast as dolphins, launched themselves up and over the hurdles in their path, then splashed gracefully back down.

"Look at them go!" Aisha said. "They're swimming even faster than before, and they're jumping so high!"

"That's the magic of confidence," Queen Aurora said.

"Wow, if the practice is this exciting, I can't wait to watch the actual Games!" said Emily.

"Please call us when they start," Aisha pleaded Aurora.

"Of course I will," said Aurora. "But I fear we might need your help again before then. Selena still has two of the lockets and we can't hold the Games without them."

"We will always help, whenever you need us," Emily promised.

They hugged Eddie, Brightblaze and Queen Aurora. "See you soon!"

Queen Aurora waggled her horn. Multi-coloured magical sparkles whooshed around the girls, and once again they felt themselves rushing through the air.

They landed exactly where they had started, behind the bookcase in the school corridor.

"Well, we've still got to do our book report," Aisha said with a sigh.

"You're not going to let standing in front of the class scare you, surely?" said Emily. "Not after everything we've been through!"

Aisha thought about it. "I'm still nervous," she said. "But I don't have to feel totally confident, do I? It's just like on the diving board. I can still do this. I just need to have my best friend by my side."

Emily smiled. "And you have."

They held hands and walked into the classroom, knowing that when best friends were together they could do anything.

The End

Join Emily and Aisha
for more fun in …
Fairtail and
the Perfect Puzzle
Read on for a sneak peek!

Aisha Khan looked at the board game boxes spread over the sitting-room floor. She sat with her best friend, Emily Turner.

"Which shall we play?" she asked.

Emily laughed. "I want to play them all!"

They had planned to practise skateboarding together after lunch, but it was pouring with rain, so Emily had raced over to Aisha's house – Enchanted Cottage – with her jacket over her head. Now they were trying to choose a game.

"What about Greedy Goat?" said Aisha,

holding up a farm-themed board game. "That was really fun last time!"

But Emily wasn't listening. She was pointing to the crystal unicorn keyring that was clipped to Aisha's belt.

"It's glowing!" said Emily.

Read
Fairtail and the Perfect Puzzle
to find out what's in store
for Aisha and Emily!

Also available

Book Nine:

Book Ten:

Book Eleven:

Book Twelve:

Look out for the next book!

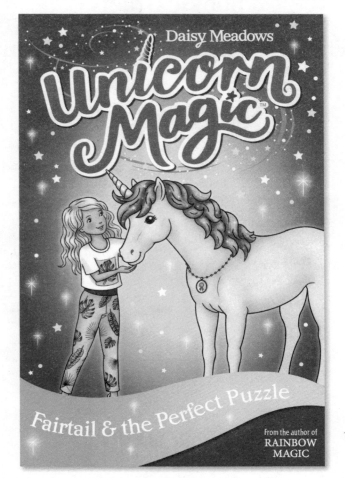

Daisy Meadows

Unicorn Magic™

Fairtail & the Perfect Puzzle

From the author of
RAINBOW
MAGIC

Visit
orchardseriesbooks.co.uk
for

✳ fun activities ✳

✳ exclusive content ✳

✳ book extracts ✳

There's something for everyone!